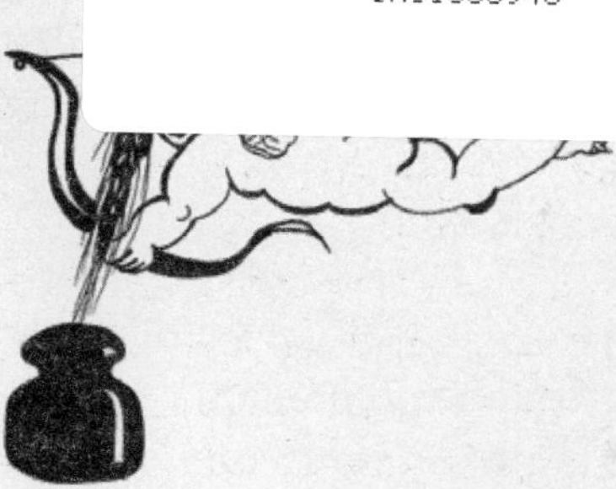

To: ______________

From: ____________

With Love

xxxx

Beryl Matthews

From tea girl to singer to credit controller, Beryl Matthews has enjoyed a variety of careers but her interest in writing has remained constant. She grew up in a family of avid readers and books have always been an important part of her life. Beryl Matthews lives in Hampshire with her husband. She is author of two Barley Books Romances

Beryl Matthews

A Christmas Crisis

To Joan,
a great pleasure
meeting you,
Beryl Matthews

SWWJ Sept 2001

Published by Barley Books Ltd 2001.

ISBN: 1902691121

Printed and bound in Great Britain by Cox & Wyman Ltd, Cardiff Road, Reading, Berkshire.

Barley Books
PO Box 103
Leeds
West Yorks
LS16 9YD.

A CHRISTMAS CRISIS

'Oh, no!' Jane Sharland stared in disbelief as the new figures appeared on the screen. The noise and bustle of the busy trading room faded, and she was conscious only of the thud of her heart as the extent of her mistake became clear. But how could she have been so wrong? All her research and instinct had told her that this was a company worth investing in; they were going places! And they certainly had, but not in the way she'd expected. The share prices had collapsed.

She gazed, unseeing, into space as she tried to grapple with the implications of this blunder, then her analytical mind clicked into action again. There was no point selling at this price, she would have to hold her nerve and wait for the New Year. The market was bound to recover then. She didn't like being so negative, but what else could she do?

'Are you all right, Jane?'

She shunted her chair over to Paula, and ran a shaking hand through her short chestnut hair. 'I'm in trouble.'

'How bad?'

'Bad enough. I think I'm in for a worrying Christmas.' She gave a grim parody of a smile. 'You know, Paula, when I started at the bank six years ago, dealing with the stock market was so exciting, but now it's becoming a nightmare. I don't think I can cope anymore.'

'Oh, come on,' her friend scolded, 'all the shares are fluctuating at the moment. With only a few days to Christmas, I expect a lot of people are cashing in for a bit of extra spending money over the holiday. It'll pick up again, and it isn't like you to let a small crisis throw you into a panic.'

'Small!' she gasped. 'the bank could lose money because of me, and you know how they hate to do that. I think it's time I retired.'

Paula laughed. 'Don't be daft, you're

only twenty-eight.'

'I feel twice that age, at least.' She stood up and tugged at her skirt, trying to cover her knees. Damn! She shouldn't have worn this suit today. After making such a mistake she needed to look poised and elegant, not like some trendy teenager. 'I'd better go and tell David.'

Her friend shrugged. 'He'll probably tell you not to worry. After all, it's not the first time this sort of thing has happened.'

'It's the first time it's happened to me,' she muttered, as she made her way to the office. Thank goodness David was a friend and someone she knew would give her helpful advice.

'Come,' a voice called in answer to her knock.

Jane stepped inside and stopped suddenly. 'Er … I was looking for David - Mr Brandon,' she corrected quickly.

The tall man who rose to greet her was a stranger, and she took an instant dislike to him. She had been expecting to see her cheerful friend, and instead she was facing a man who looked as if he had never laughed in his life.

'Brandon isn't here. You deal with me.'

She didn't care for the abrupt tone to his voice. 'And you are?'

'Devlin.' He indicated a chair near the desk. 'Sit down.'

'I prefer to stand; this won't take long,' she told him, her head coming up defiantly. She made a snap judgement; this was a man accustomed to using his height and powerful aura to intimidate, but he wasn't going to do that to her!

'As you wish.'

When he also remained standing she knew the battle lines had been drawn, and she assessed her enemy. She wasn't sure why she should feel this way about him, but the message was coming over very clearly. Perhaps it was his startling appearance. His hair was blue-black and his eyes were an unusual pale grey, almost colourless, and as cold as the icy weather outside.

'What did you want to see me about?' his gaze flicked over her left hand, '*Miss* ...?'

'Sharland.' She took a deep breath,

released it quietly and then spoke, 'I bought some stock which has taken a dive.'

'Who are they and how much are you down?'

The extraordinary eyes locked onto hers and didn't even blink when she told him. With one fluid movement he was sitting at his desk and calling up something on the computer, frowning at the information being displayed. Then he looked up. 'Do sit down - please.'

The 'please' was clearly an afterthought, and she didn't think it was a word he was very familiar with, but she obeyed. He was making her feel strangely vulnerable and she didn't like it. Usually, she was fiercely independent, used to making her own decisions, and that was why she was good at her job. At least she had been until this blunder.

After what seemed like hours, he sat back, and surveyed her thoughtfully. 'What made you think this stock was worth investing in?'

She explained her reasons, which didn't seem quite so solid now in the light of recent events, but she tried to sound positive. There wasn't any sign of reaction from the man behind the desk as he returned briefly to the computer, then he picked up the phone.

'Send Peter Rogers in here,' he demanded.

There was an oppressive silence in the room, broken only by the tapping of his pen on the large oak desk, which she found intensely irritating. When Peter arrived, the man she only knew as Devlin said sharply, 'I want you to take over all Miss Sharland's work. She's lost heavily on some stock, keep an eye on it and see what you can salvage after the holiday.'

'Just a minute!' Jane was on her feet, bristling with anger; this wasn't fair. 'It's my error and I ought to be given the chance to put things right.'

'I don't want you touching this, or any transaction, again,' he told her, and dismissed Peter with a curt nod of his head.

She was stunned, unable to believe what she was hearing. 'But why? I've got a good record and this is my first mistake.'

‘My decision has been made, Miss Sharland.’

That was it? One misjudgement was obviously too many for this arrogant man. She spun angrily on her high heels and started to walk out of the office.

‘Where do you think you’re going?’ The question was softly spoken.

Turning back she said sharply. ‘To clear out my desk.’

‘I haven’t terminated your employment. Sit down,’ he demanded.

Fury raged inside her at his peremptory tone and she was tempted to disobey him, but a quick glance at his face made her abandon the idea. She was in no position to throw her weight around at the moment, so she did as she was told, but stared at him reproachfully. ‘It sounds as if you have. You’ve just given all my work to Peter, so what am I supposed to do now?’

He turned back to the screen without answering, his long fingers flying over the keyboard, then he lifted his head and studied her. She felt like a rabbit caught in the glare of headlights, unable to move out of the danger zone.

'I see from your personnel file that you were a secretary before you joined the bank.' The pen started to tap again.

She nodded curtly and glared at the offending pen, almost smiling when he threw it down. So he'd been checking up on her, but what on earth did her past employment have to do with anything?

'Do you have any plans for Christmas? Not going abroad, or anything?'

'No.' She met his gaze, puzzled by these strange questions. 'I'm going to my parents for a couple of days, that's all.'

He gave a satisfied nod. 'Good. Cancel.'

'I can't do that!' She was about to stand up again, but his grey eyes snared hers and she remained seated. He had a special talent, she thought: he could make people obey him without saying a word. She objected to his attitude, and felt that if she was going to be dismissed then she wanted to know by whom.

'Who are you, and why has Mr Brandon suddenly disappeared?' she asked boldly.

'I'm Saul Devlin, and Mr Brandon has taken early retirement.'

'But he can't have,' she exclaimed. 'He would have told me, and anyway, he's only fifty-five and was wonderful at his job.'

'So I believe,' was the noncommittal reply.

She had an uncomfortable feeling that something was terribly wrong, and that she was being assessed and watched carefully. But why? All she'd done was invest in some stock, which had not been as sound as she'd believed.

'I have to work over the holiday,' his deep voice broke through her troubled thoughts, 'and I will need the assistance of a good secretary.'

Her head snapped up in disbelief. 'You want me to work with you?'

'Yes.' One dark eyebrow rose in query. 'You find that surprising?'

'Of course I do,' she told him scathingly. 'You believe me to be so incompetent that you've taken all my work from me, and now you're asking me to act as your secretary.'

He glanced back at the screen for a moment. 'Your references are excellent, and I'm quite desperate, or I wouldn't consider this arrangement.'

This was the last thing she had expected, or wanted, and her instinct was to get as far away from this man as possible. The thought of working for him was horrific. 'My family will be disappointed, I can't let them down,' she said quickly.

He shrugged. 'Tell them it's either that or you are unemployed.'

Ouch! That was blunt speaking. When she thought of her huge mortgage, she knew she was trapped, but still, she wanted an explanation. 'What's so important that it can't wait until after Christmas?'

'That need not concern you at the moment, but it will be necessary for me to work while everyone else is away.'

She shook her head firmly. 'I will not take on this work unless I know what I will have to do!'

His chest rose as he took in a deep breath, obviously trying to control his temper. 'All I'm asking is that you help me for a few days. Is that such an onerous task?'

Yes, she wanted to tell him, you're a most objectionable man and I don't want anything to do with you, but she managed to stop herself. 'Can't you at least tell me what you are doing here?'

He paused, as if considering his words. 'A relief manager?'

She was pleased to see he'd phrased that as a question, because no one on this earth was going to believe he was as lowly as a relief manager!

'You find this funny?' he remarked wryly.

'Wasn't I supposed to?' she asked mildly, not missing the brief flash of amusement in his eyes. There was a sense of humour lurking underneath that stern exterior, she realised. It was good to know he had at least one redeeming quality.

'I expect you to believe every word I say.' His expression dared her to argue.

She stood up suddenly, quite forgetting the short skirt until she saw his gaze sweep over her legs, then back to her face. She resisted the temptation to tug at the offending article of clothing. 'If you're looking for unquestioning obedience then you've got the wrong person!'

'Sit down, Miss Sharland.' The command was softly spoken. 'I haven't dismissed you yet, and you are hardly in a position to argue with me.'

So, she thought mutinously, as she sat again, this was going to be a battle of wills, and his was undoubtedly the stronger, but she was no weakling. She sat back, crossed her legs provocatively and gave him a cold stare. She'd been making a fool of herself by jumping up and down in an effort to get away from him, but now she was going to stay put until she found out what this was all about. 'What do you want of me?'

'I've already told you. I have a lot of work to do over the holiday period and my usual secretary is sick.'

'My shorthand is rusty and I won't be nearly good enough for you,' she protested, beginning to think that she would rather be sacked than have to face this ordeal, for that was undoubtedly what it would be.

'That doesn't matter.' He dismissed her objections with a wave of his hand. 'It's your computer skills and knowledge of the stock market I require.'

'But everything will be shut down until the New Year,' she argued, not knowing why he was insisting on this, because he clearly didn't like her, anymore than she liked him. 'Can't you explain what you will be doing? It all seems very strange to me.'

'It's unfortunate that this has happened at holiday time, but I do not have the time to wait until the New Year. I have another job to do which is also urgent.'

She frowned. 'Aren't you permanent here?'

'No, hopefully my stay will be short.' He picked up the pen again, glared at it and then threw it down.

She felt apprehensive. David had disappeared and a stranger was now giving the orders with an air of absolute authority.

'Where do your parents live?' he asked, suddenly changing the subject.

'Richmond.'

'Surrey or Yorkshire?'

'Surrey.'

'Not too far away then. Take the rest of the day off and go and tell to your family that you will be working over the holiday. Then report to me on Christmas Eve.'

'Just a minute!' she exclaimed, 'I haven't said I'll do this yet.'

One dark brow rose at her tone. 'Do you have any choice?'

No, damn him, she didn't.

Her silence obviously answered his question. 'You needn't mention our conversation to anyone here.' He gave her a smile that worried her more than his curtness.

'I can hardly tell anyone what you're doing here, because I don't know, do I? Anyway, I try not to indulge in gossip.'

'I'm pleased to hear that.' He plucked a file from the top of a heap on his desk, picked up the pen and started to scribble away.

She had clearly been dismissed, and she left the office with more haste than was necessary. She grinned to herself; another ten minutes with him in that confined space and she would have been running for cover. He certainly had a most disturbing effect upon her.

'Is it true?' Paula asked as soon as she reached her desk. 'I've just heard that David isn't here anymore.'

'That's right. Taken early retirement, the new boss has just told me.'

'That's nonsense!' Paula snorted. 'David was telling me only the other day that he intended to stay until he was sixty.'

Jane shrugged. 'He must have changed his mind.'

'What's this new man like?' Paula asked, full of curiosity.

'Oh, you know the type - tall, dark and handsome.' Jane shoved her personal belongings into a plastic bag. 'His name's Saul Devlin, and watch out for him, Paula, if you change his name around a bit you end up with Devil, and I think that's a good way to describe him.'

'That bad, eh?' Then her friend suddenly seemed to realise that Jane was emptying her desk. 'What are you doing?'

'I'm going home. He's handed all my

work over to Peter, so there's nothing for me to do.'

'I don't believe this! Isn't he going to give you a chance to redeem the situation?'

'No.' She hoisted the bag up, holding it underneath in case it slit open. 'I'm going to see my parents and forget all about this until after Christmas.'

'Have you actually been sacked?' Paula asked, worriedly.

'To be quite honest I'm not sure. I haven't been told to collect my cards yet.'

'Oh, well,' Paula looked relieved. 'You'll be reinstated after the holiday, then.'

'I might not want to be. Who knows, I might meet a handsome millionaire who will take me away from all this,' she joked. 'Have a happy Christmas everyone,' she called, and giving a cheery wave she hurried out.

'But darling, you can't be working all over the holiday!' Jane's mother looked horrified. 'Has David taken leave of his senses?

'David isn't there anymore.' She then explained what had happened.

'Did you have any idea he was going to retire?' her father asked. 'He never said anything to us the last time we saw him.'

She shook her head, feeling thoroughly bewildered. 'No. It's very odd. He had a real knack for picking the right investments, and I'm sure the bank wouldn't have wanted to lose him just yet.'

'Perhaps he had to leave suddenly because of health problems?' her mother speculated. 'I must get in touch with the dear man and see if there's anything we can do for him.'

'I phoned him yesterday,' her father told them, 'but all I got was a recorded message saying that he would not be available until after the holiday.'

'Perhaps he's gone away for Christmas, then,' her mother remarked, and then frowned in concern. 'I do hope he hasn't gone into hospital without telling us?'

Jane pursed her lips thoughtfully. 'I doubt that, he seemed fit enough to me, and it was a shock seeing this other man sitting at his desk.'

'And he's asked you to work for him?' Her father pushed the cat off his chair and sat down quickly, sighing when the large bundle of black and white fur leapt onto his knees.

Jane laughed at his look of resignation. 'Well, it is Bonzo's chair, Dad.'

'No it isn't, it's mine, but I can't seem to make the pesky animal understand that.'

Bonzo circled a couple of times, then lay down, resting his chin on his paws and vibrating contentedly.

'You can't miss Christmas dinner.' Her mother returned to the vexing question. 'If we don't have it until eight in the evening, you should be finished by then, surely? You can't work all night!'

'I don't know. This man is an unknown quantity, and he told me to cancel Christmas.'

'I'm sure he didn't mean that.' Her mother dismissed the idea. 'Tell him you can't possibly work in the evenings. It isn't far from London to here and you could easily come for a few hours and stay the night with us.'

'I can't. I don't want to lose my job until I've had a chance to find another position. I've got my mortgage to pay,' she pointed out.

'We'll help you with that.' Her father smiled understandingly. 'You don't have to worry about money. We've told you that often enough.'

'I know, Dad,' she looked at him affectionately, 'but I've got to make my own way in life.'

He gave a resigned shrug. They'd had this discussion many times before. 'You're too independent, my girl.'

'Bring this man with you,' her mother interrupted, looking pleased with herself. 'He can't go without a festive meal, either.'

'What!' She was startled. 'You want to feed him?'

'Why not?'

Jane started to laugh uncontrollably. 'Oh,' she gasped, 'I can just imagine his reaction.'

'You said he was going on to another job after this one, so he's probably staying in an hotel, and I should think he'd be pleased to have a nice home- cooked meal. Ask him, and if he refuses then come on your own,' her mother persisted.

'No,' Jane spluttered, 'it will be a waste of time and I certainly don't want him here.'

Her father looked puzzled. 'What's wrong with him?'

'He's arrogant, overbearing, dictatorial …' Jane ticked the qualities off on her fingers, '… rude, sarcastic, sure of himself, intimidating and moves like a predatory animal.'

'Really? He sounds interesting, doesn't he, Dad?'

'Interesting isn't how I'd describe him,' she told them.

'No, well, dear, that's obvious.' Her mother picked up a pad and pen. 'Let's see, that will make ten for dinner, eleven counting Bonzo …'

The cat lifted his head and licked his lips in approval.

'And we've got enough food to feed twice that many,' her father remarked, dryly.

His wife ignored him. 'Then we must have a small present for them all-'

'Mum! You're wasting your time, I'm not going to ask him!'

'Don't you worry about it, dear, I'll arrange everything.'

'Mother! Don't you dare! We don't even know him,' she protested firmly, well knowing her mother's tendency to interfere. 'He will be embarrassed.'

'Of course he won't, dear. A man like that will handle any situation with ease.'

'How do you know that?' Jane never ceased to be amazed at her mother's reasoning.

'From your very graphic description of him, of course.'

'I don't believe this,' she muttered under her breath.

'I'll find him something nice. What kind of tie does he like?' she asked, ignoring the scowl on her daughter's face.

'I don't know!'

Her mother continued writing. 'Never mind. How old is he?'

'What difference does that make?' This conversation was ridiculous.

'A lot. Is he young or old?' she persisted.

'In his thirties, I suppose. I can't say I've given it much thought.'

'Ah, well, he'll want something elegant and not too flashy. I know just the shop.' She gave a satisfied smile and wrote something down.

Jane's mouth dropped open and she shot her father a disbelieving look.

'No point arguing,' he told her quietly. 'She's made her mind up.'

Her mother put the pad in her handbag ready for the shopping trip. 'I look forward to meeting him.'

'What did you say his name was?' Her father dumped the cat on the floor, much to the disgust of the animal.

'Saul Devil … sorry, Devlin.' She couldn't help thinking of him as Devil; the name suited him admirably.

'I seem to know the name.' Her father tapped his head as if trying to bring the information to the surface. 'But I can't think where I've heard it before.'

'It'll come to you,' his wife assured him, then turned back to her daughter. 'That's settled then, we'll see you some time before eight.'

'I'll try, but I'll phone if I can't make it.'

'But you must! Andrew's coming for the day and he'll be disappointed if you're not here.'

'Why did you do that?' She groaned. 'You know I've broken off our engagement.'

'Well, I'm sure he still loves you.' Her mother looked at her pointedly. 'I could hardly invite his parents and leave him out, could I? And he's such a nice boy.'

'But why did you invite any of them?' she asked, thoroughly exasperated. What a Christmas this was turning out to be!

'Because we always do,' her mother told her reasonably, 'and I saw no reason to change things this year just because you and Andrew are having a temporary disagreement.'

Jane sighed inwardly. Her mother

refused to accept that she was finished with Andrew, and couldn't understand why her daughter wanted to live and work in London, with all the travelling and stress, when she could settle down and raise grandchildren for them.

She gave her father another appealing look for support, but he was too busy trying to thwart Bonzo's efforts to regain control of the chair. The cat had jumped onto the arm, forced himself behind her father, and with four feet braced against the back of the chair, was pushing with all his strength to try and dislodge him.

'I'll expect you here for our family Christmas dinner?' her mother stated, obviously unwilling to let the subject drop.

'I'll do my best, Mum.' She knew there was little point arguing further.

By now, both man and cat were swearing.

'Don't tease the animal,' her mother scolded.

At that moment, the cat gave a yell of triumph as her father stood up. Bonzo, looking smug, stretched across the hastily vacated seat, rolled over and stuck four white feet into the air.

Her father scowled. ‘I’m going for a walk, and I think I’ll buy myself a dog,’ he threatened.

‘Morning, Miss Sharland.’ The doorkeeper rushed to unlock the inner door for her. ‘You involved with that lot upstairs, then?’

‘Lot?’ she asked frowning. ‘There’s only Mr Devlin, isn’t there?’

‘No, Miss. There’s four of them altogether.’ He rubbed his chin thoughtfully. ‘They’ve made a right mess of my holiday, I can tell you. The wife’s not at all happy. Do you know what’s going on?’

‘I haven’t got a clue.’ She hurried to the lift. But she was certainly going to find out.

Saul Devlin looked pointedly at his watch as Jane walked into the office.

‘I’m not late, it isn’t even nine yet,’ she pointed out. Then she noticed that he had shed his jacket, loosened his tie and rolled up the sleeves of his pristine white shirt. ‘Heavens! You look as if you’ve been here all night.'

'I've been here since seven,' he snapped. 'So, as you've finally arrived, let's get on with things. There's a lot to do.'

He swept past her, heading for the door. 'Oh, oh,' she muttered under her breath, 'who's had a bad night, then?'

He heard her, stopped abruptly and spun round. 'Yes I have. Hotel beds are always too short for me and some fools were having a noisy party until three this morning.'

'Well, it is the festive season,' she reminded him.

'Not for us!' He bent until his eyes were level with hers. 'So don't rattle my cage, Miss Sharland, or I might bite.'

Jane recoiled slightly at the deep growl in his voice. And this was the man her mother wanted to ask over for Christmas dinner? She sincerely hoped that idea had been forgotten!

'Come and meet the team.' He strode away and she had no option but to follow.

She was introduced to two men and one woman, Kath, John and Harry.

'Roped you in as well, has he?' they laughed.

Saul didn't seem to find the joke funny. 'Miss Sharland-'

'Jane,' she corrected. For some odd reason she wasn't scared of him now, and if she had to work over the holiday then she wanted the atmosphere as friendly as possible.

He sighed. 'Jane worked as a dealer with the bank, so she knows the business, and I want this job finished by the New Year, if not earlier.'

The three saluted smartly and scuttled back to their places in mock terror.

As he started to return to his office, she asked, 'What do you want me to do?'

'Your first job will be to organise some food for us,' he told her, still walking away. 'I don't want to stop for meals today.'

There was a collective groan, which he ignored.

He looked over his shoulder. 'Find a restaurant who would be prepared to deliver.'

'Who's paying?' she asked, knowing

that this wasn't going to be easy to arrange on Christmas Eve, and could prove rather expensive.

'I am, and I don't want sandwiches or pizza.' Then he disappeared into his office.

'In that case I know just the place. Very expensive,' she added gleefully, and picked up the phone.

When that was done, she went over to Kath. 'What shall I do now?'

'You'll have to ask Saul.'

Jane grimaced and Kath chuckled at her expression. 'I see you don't like him, but don't be fooled by his stern exterior, there's a very nice man underneath.'

'You could have fooled me.' She peered at the printouts on the desk. 'What are you looking for?'

Everyone stopped work and looked at her.

'You mean you don't know what we're doing here?' asked Harry, obviously surprised.

She shook her head. 'No, I was just ordered to turn up.'

'I expect he'll explain later,' Kath

assured her.

Jane saw the raised eyebrows as they'd glanced at each other before engrossing themselves in their work again. As they were obviously not going to enlighten her, she headed for the office and put her head through the open door. 'Lunch will be served at twelve,' she announced. 'What is my next task?'

Saul picked up a pile of papers and held them out to her. 'Find yourself a word processor and type these for me.'

She quickly read the top page to see if she could decipher his writing. The bold style was quite legible and as she read realisation dawned at last! She should have known right from the start, but she'd been so concerned about her own mistake … 'You're an investigator!'

'Ah,' he sat back and folded his arms. 'I wondered how long it was going to take you.'

'Is the bank in trouble?' Was that why David had left so suddenly?

'No, but one or two of the employees might be.'

It was a rather subdued Jane who worked for the next few hours, but thankfully, the report she was working on didn't relate to this bank. It was concerned with his last job and she couldn't help being impressed with his thoroughness, and the evidence he had uncovered would stand up in any court of law, she guessed. The man was good at his job. Dishonesty was abhorrent to her but she went cold as she realised that he was now checking up on her colleagues.

'Take a break.' Kath placed a mug of coffee in front of her.

'Thanks.' She sat back, rubbed her temple and groaned. 'I should be having a good time with my family instead of being here. Why does this have to be done now? What has Saul Devlin got against Christmas?'

Kath perched on the end of her desk. 'When he's called in on a job like this, he likes to have the place to himself if possible. And anyway, this is a bad time of the year for him; I think he'd rather work.'

'Why?' She couldn't understand why

anyone would want to do that. She loved this time of the year.

'His wife died suddenly two years ago and he hasn't been the same man since.'

'Oh, how dreadful.' Jane felt awful about the nasty things she'd said and thought about him. She really must stop making snap judgements about people. 'What happened?'

'A massive stroke. They'd only been married eighteen months and I think he was devastated.'

'He must have loved her very much.'

Kath nodded. 'I believe that the only way he could deal with it was by work, work and more work.'

'He obviously still hasn't come to terms with the loss, even after two years.' Jane remarked sadly.

'Oh I'm sure he has, but work has become a habit.' Kath stood up and looked at Jane thoughtfully. 'What he needs is a lovely woman who will shake him up and show him that life can be fun.'

It was ten o'clock before Jane finally

reached her apartment that evening, and although she was tired, she didn't think she would be able to sleep. The revelation about Saul Devlin's private life had touched her greatly and she was determined to make him laugh … well maybe that was asking rather too much, she thought, but another one of those appealing smiles would be a start.

A trip to the all night supermarket was the first part of her plan, and by midnight she had everything ready. Christmas Day was going to be fun, whether he liked it or not! She was feeling reckless and strangely happy, which was amazing considering that she might well have lost her job.

'Here, let me help you with those.' The doorkeeper rushed to her aid. 'What have you got here?'

'Food.' She grinned, 'you can join us upstairs if you like, I've got plenty.'

'No thanks, Miss. I've just got to let you in, then I can go. Mr Devlin is going to lock up tonight. But I'll give you a hand with all this before I leave.'

‘Thanks.’

They loaded the boxes into the lift, and as they made their way up, Jane looked at the amount she’d bought and wondered if she’d overdone it. When Saul Devlin saw all this, he was liable to blow a fuse, never mind smile, and he probably wouldn’t approve of the dress she was wearing, either. It wasn’t low cut or provocative, the sleeves were long, the neckline high and the skirt reached to mid calf, but the soft emerald green material clung to her slender curves and swirled around her legs, the colour accentuating her green eyes. Still she didn’t care! Christmas was a time for giving, a time to share and a time to be happy.

Kath, John and Harry, rushed to help when they saw her struggling with the packages.

‘What have you got here?’ Kath asked, clearing a table to make room for everything.

‘We might have to work, but we’re going to make this a festive day.’ Jane began to unpack and lay everything out.

She'd bought cold meats, salad, nuts, sausage rolls, fruit, mince pies, Christmas cake; in fact everything you could imagine, including one bottle of very good wine and some crackers.

'What's going on here?' asked a quiet voice behind her. Then he stepped forward, picked up the wine and frowned. 'I don't want you the worse for drink today.'

'It's only one bottle!' she protested, deciding that her sympathy for him yesterday had been misplaced. He was a miserable devil after all. 'There will be enough for one small glass for each of us, and I've got orange juice for anyone who wants it.'

He still didn't look happy, but she was determined to break through his defences today. Diving down into one of the boxes she pulled out a sprig of mistletoe and held it over Kath. 'Come on then, wish her a happy Christmas.'

Harry and John did so amid much laughter, and even Saul kissed his colleague gently on the cheek. Good, thought Jane. That was a start.

Harry took the sprig from Jane's hand, held it over her and gave her a kiss; John did same, then turned to Saul, his face alight with amusement. 'Your turn.'

At first she thought he was going to refuse, but after only the slightest hesitation he stepped forward, and without touching her lowered his head. She turned her head expecting a brief kiss on the cheek, but he caught hold of her chin and made her face him. The kiss was firm and as his lips moved sensuously over hers, the feeling was like nothing she had ever experienced before. Her senses were being bombarded and she began to lose her grip on reality; all she was conscious of was the warmth coming from his powerful body, the slight smell of a tangy after-shave, and many other things she was incapable of defining. Her reaction to his embrace robbed her of breath.

When he stepped away she was disappointed and shocked to discover that she had wanted more than that brief kiss - much more!

They gazed at each other for a moment,

then Saul raised his eyebrows with an unspoken question. But what had happened in those few seconds was a mystery to her, as well.

'Now let's get some work done,' he said, turning on his heel and heading for the office.

Kath was grinning at her. 'Well done, Jane. For a moment there he looked like the man we first knew.'

'Have you known him long?' she asked, talking to give herself time to drag herself back into the real world.

'Six years.' Kath picked up a small sausage roll and popped it into her mouth.

'And he's good at his job, is he?'

'The best.' She chewed and swallowed. 'Firms bring him in because they know he'll find the culprit, however deeply the evidence is buried.'

Jane felt a shiver of apprehension go through her. 'Does he think David Brandon has been involved in fraud?'

'Oh, we won't know anything for sure until the investigation is complete, but they don't usually call us in unless there is a very strong suspicion of something being wrong.'

'Jane!'

Kath chuckled. 'The master calls you.'

She went into the office and looked around in disgust. David had always kept this place spotless and without a thing out of place, but now the huge desk was littered with empty plastic cups, and there were files and print-outs scattered all over the pale blue carpet, as if he'd been on his hands and knees examining them. She bent to pick some up and place them on a chair.

'Leave those, I know exactly what I'm doing,' he told her sharply.

Without a word she dropped them back onto the floor. She had been wondering how he would treat her after that shattering kiss, but he appeared to be completely unaffected, which was more than she could say about her own emotions - they were in turmoil.

'You did a good job with those reports yesterday,' he complimented, 'and today I'd like you to start on this.'

He handed her a huge pile of handwritten notes and she sighed. 'Gosh! This will take for ever.'

'No it won't, you're an excellent typist. Start with those and let me know when you've finished.'

'Is this the work from here?' she asked, chewing her lip anxiously.

'Yes, but you needn't look so worried, it's just some preliminary notes.'

She returned to her desk and dumped the pile of paper down. Preliminary notes! No wonder he needed a secretary.

Saul kept her busy all morning, stopping her often to find something for them, or to replenish the coffee percolator.

'You drink too much caffeine,' she scolded once, when he refilled his mug for the umpteenth time.

'I know,' he said, taking a large gulp of the hot liquid.

At one point in the morning they all went into a huddle at the other end of the office, talking softly so she couldn't hear them. I am beginning to feel like a pariah, she thought mutinously, pounding the keyboard with unnecessary force. Saul wasn't giving her anything important to do, she was only running errands and typing, so what on earth was she doing here?

'Let's take a break and enjoy this lovely spread Jane has provided for us, shall we?' Kath came and stood beside her desk and smiled warmly. 'It all looks very inviting.'

The next hour was enjoyable and Jane began to relax in the friendly atmosphere. What was she worrying about? It wasn't as if she had a guilty conscience. All she'd done was buy some stock, which had not come up to expectations and that wasn't a crime … was it?

She watched Saul, sitting on a desk with a plate piled high with food and a drop of wine in a paper cup. He was talking in a friendly way with them all and looked almost human. As soon as they'd eaten, however, he soon had everyone working again.

Jane was so busy that the afternoon flew by, and about six o'clock she sat back, rubbed her tired eyes, and glanced around the large trading room. It was strange to see it empty like this, and the silence was unnatural - no phones ringing, no voices raised and no one hurrying around.

'That's enough for today,' Saul announced. 'You might as well go home and try to salvage something of the holiday, but I want you all here again tomorrow.'

Kath, Harry and John left with great speed, and Jane began to pack up the remnants of the food.

'Thank you for going to so much trouble today.' Saul came up and started to help her. 'It was greatly appreciated. You must tell me what it cost and I'll reimburse you.'

'I don't want anything. It was my gift to you all.' Why did he have to spoil the compliment by offering her money? But she was pleased to see he didn't insist, he merely nodded and dropped the subject.

'What are you going to do?' she asked, remembering her mother's insistence that he join them for dinner.

'Stay here for a while, then go back to the hotel.' He didn't look too enamoured with the idea, and ran his hand distractedly through his hair. 'Unless …?'

Jane's insides lurched. Her mother hadn't, had she?

'I had a phone call from your mother today.' He picked up the piece of mistletoe, fingered it thoughtfully, and then tossed it into the box. 'She invited me over for dinner tonight.'

She had! Just wait until she saw her on her own. This was so embarrassing.

'I refused, of course.'

Jane sagged in relief. 'I'm sorry about that, but when my mother gets an idea in her head, it's a job to stop her.'

He gave a half smile. 'Your mother sounded very determined and I did feel as if I was being forced into accepting.'

'Oh, I know exactly what she's like.' She lifted a box and tucked it under her arm. 'But she doesn't mean any harm, she just likes people and the more around her, the better.'

'She doesn't even know me, though, and you must admit that it was a strange thing to do. She chatted away to me as if I was a lifelong friend.'

'And I expect she tried to find out what

you were doing here?' she groaned.

'Yes, she was most concerned about Brandon.' He paused for a moment. 'Is he a friend of your family's?'

'We've known him for some years and he often used to come round for a meal.' She looked up at him imploringly. 'Is he in trouble?'

Saul shrugged and looked away, picking up the other box. 'We don't know anything for sure yet, but he was in charge so he had to leave until the investigation is complete.'

'You mean he might be able to come back after this is over?' she asked eagerly.

'No, he has decided to take early retirement, that is true, Jane.' He pulled a bunch of keys from his pocket, checked them and then put them back.

'Oh, I see.' But she didn't really, and knew that he was holding back from revealing the details.

They made their way downstairs in silence, and as she waited for him to lock the main doors, she looked around at the empty streets, and shivered as a blast of cold wind caught her hair.

'I don't suppose you've ever seen the city this quiet, have you?' he asked, pocketing the keys.

She shook her head and laughed. 'No, it doesn't seem natural. But then, I've never been in the business centre at holiday times.'

'Let's get out of this icy weather.' He took hold of her arm and guided her towards the car park.

When they reached her car, she opened the boot and they dumped the boxes inside, then she smiled at him. 'Thank you. I'll see you tomorrow.'

He leaned against the side of the car and looked down at her. 'About your mother's invitation ...'

'Oh, you needn't worry about that,' she dismissed with a laugh, cursing her mother for putting them both in this awkward position. 'I know what she was up to, she thought that you would be more likely to let me off early if you were coming to dinner, as well.'

'Ah.' He looked thoughtful then gave

her a smile, which rocked her back on her heels. 'I must admit that I don't relish the thought of spending Christmas night at the hotel, so do you think I could change my mind?'

'You mean you want to come?' she gasped in disbelief.

'Your mother was most insistent,' he said, dryly.

Jane, thoroughly disconcerted by his acceptance, fumbled for her mobile phone. 'I'm sure it will be all right. I'll just let them know we're on our way.'

Her father answered. 'Tell Mum Mr Devlin will be coming, and we'll be there about seven thirty.'

'That's wonderful.' He called the news to his wife, who was obviously in the kitchen. 'Oh, by the way, Jane, I've remembered where I heard Devlin's name before. He's a trouble-shooter, with a fierce and ruthless reputation.'

'So I've found out, Dad.'

'Do you know who he's after?'

'No, sorry.' She couldn't go into this with the man in question standing beside her. 'We'll see you soon.'

'It won't take long to get to Richmond this evening, there shouldn't be much traffic around,' she told him. 'Do you want to come in my car, or will you follow me?'

'I'll follow.'

*   *   *

The house was ablaze with Christmas lights in the front windows, and inside a huge tree stood in the corner of the spacious room, and around the base was a pile of brightly coloured parcels. There was a real log fire burning in the grate, and Jane began to relax in the atmosphere of warmth and love. She loved this old house, perched on the top of Richmond Hill, close to the park and terraces and overlooking the Thames. Her mother had let her enthusiasm run away with her again, she noted, and wondered if she had gone ahead and bought Saul a present. She sincerely hoped not!

'Ah, Saul.' Her mother bustled up to them, a great big smile on her still pretty face. 'We are so pleased you could join us after all. Let me introduce you to everyone.'

Saul was welcomed with all the warmth her family was capable of - and that was a great deal. Jane was fortunate to have been surrounded with so
much affection all her life, and she couldn't help wondering what his life was like out of work. Was he as solitary as he appeared?'

She watched his progress around the room and couldn't help noticing that her father was regarding him warily. She must ask him later what he had found out about him.

At that moment, Andrew came up and insisted on kissing her, too possessively, she thought. She had returned his ring some months ago, so he no longer had any claim on her, and to kiss her so ardently in front of everyone was far too familiar. She tried not to compare him with Saul but on a scale of one to ten, he scored no more than three.

'Boyfriend?' Saul murmured in her ear, when Andrew had dashed off to get someone a drink.

'Ex fiancé,' she said forcibly, still

rattled by Andrew's behaviour, and was surprised to hear Saul give a deep chuckle.

Well, she thought rather breathlessly, she'd set out to coax a smile from him, but she had got more than she'd bargained for. She had started to see a different man today, and she liked him. Far too much for her comfort.

During dinner she found it difficult to keep her eyes off Saul, much to Andrew's disgust.

'Who is he?' he asked, peevishly.

'Saul Devlin.'

'I know his name,' he said sharply. 'What does he do and how do you know him?'

'He works at the bank … he's taken David Brandon's place.' She was not prepared to elaborate further, and objected to him acting the jealous lover.

'And you invited him for Christmas dinner?' he asked, glaring at the man in question.

'No, mother did.'

'Why?'

She felt like snapping that it was none of

his business, but didn't want to spoil the party atmosphere, so she swallowed her irritation. 'When Mum heard that we'd be working right over the holiday period, she told me to bring him home with me. You know what she's like.' Jane glanced at her mother and smiled. 'She's got so much love to give and wants everyone to have some.'

'Yes, she's a lovely lady,' he agreed. 'Your father's a lucky man.'

'He knows it, even if he doesn't show his feelings.'

'You take after him, don't you?' He stared moodily into his wine glass.

Now was her chance! 'Yes, I think I do.' She reached out and touched his hand. 'I'm not the one for you, Andrew. I know our families would like us to marry, but it wouldn't be right. We'd make each other miserable.'

He grimaced and took her hand in his. 'I've been giving it a lot of thought lately and I think you're right, but I do care for you Jane, and if there was still a chance ...?'

'There isn't, Andrew,' she told him as

gently as possible. 'I'm fond of you, but we've known each other for such a long time, and quite honestly I think of you as the brother I never had. I'd be so happy if you would find yourself a gentle girl who would love you and give you children.'

'Well,' he bent to whisper in her ear confidentially, 'I met a smashing girl last month and I've taken her out a couple of times. We get on well together, seem to have the same interests.'

Jane beamed in relief. 'That's wonderful.'

He nodded, then cast a glance at Saul. 'I don't like the look of that man, Jane. I hope you're not in love with him?'

'Er … no.'

'You don't sound too sure.'

She glanced at Saul who was deep in conversation with her father and uncle, and bit back a sigh. 'He's a very complex man and I can't decide how I feel about him. When we first met I couldn't stand the sight of him, but now I know him better, I'm not sure.' She gave a rather helpless shrug. Since she'd walked into his office, her life had changed in some way she couldn't fathom. He was playing havoc with her emotions.

Andrew refilled her wine glass, a deep frown on his face. 'You be careful of him, Jane, he looks like trouble to me.'

'You don't have to worry, I'm quite capable of looking out for myself.' And she hoped that statement was true in this case. She was usually focused and positive about the future, but now she was confused, and she didn't like the feeling.

'We'll have coffee in the other room,' her mother announced, breaking her train of thought, for which she was grateful. It was Christmas, for goodness sake, and she was with her family and friends, so what on earth was she fretting about?

When they were settled, each guest was given a present and her mother glowed with pleasure as the parcels were opened. Jane had an exquisite jade necklace from her parents, her father had a laptop computer, and the rest of them received everything from mobile phones to glossy books on any subject they were interested in. These were her mother's idea of small gifts.

Her father fished a large parcel out from behind the tree and handed it to his wife, who exclaimed in delight when she saw the soft leather jacket and new handbag her husband and daughter had given her.

Jane turned her attention back to Saul and watched him open his package. If he was surprised or uncomfortable, he didn't show it. Instead, he looked up and smiled at her mother.

'Thank you, Mrs Sharland, you have excellent taste, this is just the kind of tie I would have bought for myself.' And as if to emphasise the point, he removed the tie he was wearing and put it on, rolling the other one up and slipping it into his pocket.

It was a gracious gesture and Jane knew her mother would appreciate it.

The gathering was lively. They were all well fed and obviously enjoying each other's company, and Jane was just looking for an empty space to put her cup down when she saw a black tail with a white blob on the end stalking past her. She watched as Bonzo sat in the middle of the carpet and looked at each guest in turn, picking the most comfortable lap in the room. His gaze locked onto Saul and he went and sat in front of him.

Jane watched in amusement as man and cat tried to stare each other out, and thought, you're wasting your time there, Bonzo. But the animal had picked his victim well, and she watched Saul's mouth twitch at the corners, then he tapped his knees and the cat was up in a flash, gazing at him in adoration.

The rest of the evening flew by and she was surprised to see it was twelve thirty when Saul made a move to leave.

When he'd said goodbye to everyone, he turned to Jane. 'You'll see me out and point me in the right direction?'

'I'll get my car and guide you onto the main road,' she said, grabbing her coat.

'That won't be necessary. You stay with your family, I'll find my own way.'

'If you're sure?' When he nodded she followed him outside. The night was clear and the wind had dropped, but there was a sharp frost and she rubbed her hands together to keep them warm. 'Be careful of the roads, they might be a bit slippery.'

'I will. Thank you, Jane,' he said, unlocking the door and turning to face her. 'I've had a most enjoyable evening.'

'I'm glad you came.'

When he reached out and pulled her into his arms, she melted into his embrace as if it was the most natural thing in the world for her to do. The kiss was nothing like the gentle controlled one she had received in the office. This was full of passion and a sensuality that made her head reel.

He pulled away from her, his breath forming small clouds in the cold night air, and ran the back of his hand down her face, hardly touching her. Then without a word he got into his car.

'Are you over the limit?' she asked, suddenly gathering her scrambled thoughts together. 'I should have asked before this.'

'No,' he said softly, 'I've only had one glass of wine. I'm quite sober.'

She shoved her hands into her pockets and watched him pull out into the road. So, he hadn't kissed her like that because he'd had too much to drink - he'd been fully aware of what he'd been doing. And she'd forgotten to give him directions, but again, he obviously knew where he was going because he'd driven off the right way.

The rest of their guests began to spill out, and when she'd waved them off, she went back into the house.

'What a charming man,' her mother exclaimed, before she'd hardly had time to get inside the door. 'I told him he was welcome to come back with you tomorrow, if he wanted to.'

Jane hung her coat in the hall. 'And what did he say?'

He thanked me and said he would have to see how the work went before making a decision. Do you want a hot drink before going to bed?'

'No thanks.' Jane walked into the lounge and sat in front of the fire.

'Can't think why you don't like him.' Her mother followed her. 'Such a nice man, isn't he Dad?'

'Maybe, but from what I've heard, he

isn't the sort to get on the wrong side of. I tried to find out what he was doing at the bank, but he wouldn't say a word.'

'Of course he wouldn't, dear,' his wife said. 'His work would be confidential, and anyway, I don't know what you're worrying about, it hasn't got anything to do with our Jane.'

'I know that, but I was curious, that's all.'

'He comes from Edinburgh,' her mother told them, 'that's why he's staying in London and working over the Christmas holiday. He'll celebrate at Hogmanay, he told me.'

'Ah.' Jane gave a sleepy smile. 'I thought there was a trace of an accent, but I couldn't pin it down.'

'And Bonzo likes him.' Her mother started to bustle around picking up glasses and plates. 'Cats are very intuitive, you know.'

Her father sighed wearily and stood up. 'Leave the clearing up until the morning.'

'I can't do that, I won't be able to get into the kitchen if I leave everything like this.'

He turned to his daughter. 'Well, you'd better get some sleep if you're going to be fit for work in the morning.'

Jane wasn't sure she was going to get much sleep. She felt far too keyed up, and she caught hold of her father's arm just as he made to follow his wife into the kitchen.

'What did you find out about him, Dad?'

'Only that he's good at his job, too good some would say, and completely ruthless. Anyone who has done the slightest thing wrong gets no mercy from him.'

Now she was certain she wouldn't get any sleep tonight.

The next day Jane swept into the office loaded with food again. Provided by her mother this time.

'Good Morning,' she called.

John clutched his head. 'Must you shout so?'

She chuckled, they all looked rather bleary eyed. 'Had a rough night?'

There was a collective groan as she

started to clear a table and lay out the food.

'You're not expecting us to eat today, are you?' Kath asked, eyeing the rich food with distaste.

'Oh dear me.' Jane shook her head in amusement. 'You are all in a state, aren't you? Would you like some coffee?'

'Please.' They spoke in unison.

'Where's Saul?' After last night she felt quite entitled to use his first name.

'In his office.'

'Right.' She looked through the open door. 'Morning. Would you like tea or coffee?'

'Tea, please.' He was frowning and looked up briefly. 'Where did you put that last report you typed for me?'

'It's on the chair behind you, there wasn't room on your desk for it.'

'Thanks.' He swung his chair round, picked it up and spun back to the desk again, without glancing at her again.

'Oh, you're wearing the tie Mum gave you.' She knew her mother would be pleased.

'I like it and it was kind of her to invite

me, I enjoyed the evening.' He gave a slight smile. 'Much better than being on my own in the hotel.'

'Jane!' someone bellowed from outside. 'I thought we were going to get some coffee?'

'Oops!' She rolled her eyes. 'Someone isn't too happy this morning.' But Saul wasn't listening; he was concentrating on something and frowning again.

It was about eleven when Jane picked up on the change in atmosphere. She watched them all disappear into Saul's office, and was surprised to see the door close behind them. He never shut his office door!

Half an hour later it opened and everyone filed out looking very serious. Saul came and stood beside her and she smiled up at him.

'We won't need you any more, Jane; go and spend the rest of the holiday with your family.'

She couldn't hide her surprise or dismay at this unexpected announcement. 'But you said I was to work for you until the New

Year.'

'I know, but that is no longer necessary.' He held her gaze for a few seconds, then looked away. 'Do as I say and don't argue, Jane.'

The disappointment was crushing. In the short time she'd know him her feelings had turned from dislike to love, and she wanted to stay near him. 'I don't understand.'

'We shall be winding up the investigation soon.'

He turned to walk away but she leapt to her feet and stood in front of him. 'You've found something?'

'Yes.' He looked at her hand on his arm and stepped back a pace.

That small gesture hurt! She didn't like to ask what they had discovered; after all it wasn't any of her business. 'Mum invited you again this evening,' she said, unwilling to believe she wouldn't see him again, 'will you be able to find the house again?'

'I won't be coming,' he told her briskly. 'I've already phoned your mother to let her know.'

He turned and walked back into the office. She couldn't believe that this was the same man who had kissed her so ardently last night. What had happened to make him revert back to the Saul Devlin she had met the first time?

She slipped on her coat and picked up her bag. That kiss had meant so much to her, but it obviously hadn't touched him. She wandered over to Kath berating herself for being such a fool.

'I'll leave you to clear up what's left of the food.'

Kath looked up, her expression guarded, 'OK, thanks for everything, Jane, enjoy the rest of your holiday.'

She nodded gloomily and was about to leave when something caught her attention. She picked up the computer printout and gasped. 'Wow! Someone bought the same shares as me, and a huge amount, as well. They're going to lose a fortune.'

'Are they, Jane?' Saul was standing behind her.

'Well of course they are. Who bought them?'

'Brandon.'

'David? But he would never make a mistake like that.' She shook the printout in amazement. 'He knew the market better than anyone.'

'Exactly.'

She gazed at Saul's grim face and was sure her heart stopped beating for a moment. 'What do you mean?'

'He's either very lucky … or …' He shrugged expressively. '… or he knows something,' she finished the sentence for him and leaned on the desk for support. The blood was pounding in her ears. 'Are you talking about insider dealing?'

'Yes.'

'But David wouldn't do such a thing,' she persisted, unable to believe what she was hearing. 'It's a criminal offence!'

'It certainly is.' Saul turned and walked away.

Jane watched his retreating figure, then pushed herself away from the desk and hurtled after him. 'Are you dismissing me because I bought the same stock?' Her voice was a whisper.

He didn't answer her questions but his silence was ominous, making her insides churn in fear.

'Your work here is finished, now will you please go home?'

She caught hold of his sleeve. 'Is that company going to make a sudden recovery - a take-over, or something?'

The look he gave her was impossible to read and she fought with rising panic. 'You think I'm implicated in this, don't you? That's why you kept me here, under the pretence of working for you. You weren't sure, but now you are?'

'Don't jump to conclusions. I can't discuss this with you - you know that. Now go to your family and stay there while I complete my investigation.'

She didn't know this cold man staring at her without a glint of warmth in his pale eyes, and she didn't want to know him. He frightened her. 'I swear to you …' her voice shook, 'I'd never do anything like that.'

For a moment his gaze softened and without thinking, he reached out to touch her face, but then his hand dropped abruptly and he walked away, slamming his office door shut.

Jane stumbled out, too shocked to say goodbye to the others.

He thought she was a criminal!

'Hello, darling.' Her father put his newspaper down. 'We weren't expecting you until this evening.'

'I know. Where's Mum?'

'Gone to see your Aunt Grace.' He studied her face. 'What's the matter, don't you feel well?'

She sat down and when Bonzo jumped onto her lap she started to run her hand over his silky fur. The animal was warm and purring contentedly and Jane found it comforting.

'I've been dismissed,' she said, not taking her eyes off the cat.

'That's a bit sudden, isn't it?'

She lifted her head then. 'I'm under investigation.'

Her father started to grin as if it was a joke, but the amusement faded almost immediately. 'You're serious?'

She nodded, then explained what had happened. 'How could he believe I would do such a terrible thing?' she whispered, unable to hide her distress.

'Jane.' Her father sat beside her and took hold of her hands, ignoring the quick swipe the cat gave him as the stroking stopped. 'Has Saul told you that you are under suspicion?'

'Well, no, not exactly.' She chewed her lip anxiously. 'But it was obvious what he was thinking.'

'I'm sure you haven't anything to be worried about,' her father comforted. 'You've always said David had an uncanny knack for picking the right shares, well it was obviously too good and has raised the bank's suspicions. But your record is clear and the fact that you bought the same stock as he did is a coincidence - nothing more.'

'I know that, Dad, but Saul doesn't believe me.' That thought hurt more than she was willing to admit.

'He has a fierce reputation, but after meeting him I'm sure he's a fair man. He will clear your name.' He patted her hand comfortingly.

'But my name doesn't need clearing!' she protested. 'I haven't done anything wrong.'

'We know that, darling, but Saul Devlin has a job to do and must look into everything carefully, however tenuous the connection with David's criminal activities. I'm told he's extremely thorough and will soon find out that you acted innocently.'

'But why didn't he let me stay and help. I could have answered all his questions.' She paused a moment and blinked back a tear. 'I'm frightened, Dad.'

He squeezed her hand. 'He probably has a good reason for sending you away. We've just got to trust him ...'

'Trust who?' Her mother breezed in.

Jane left the explaining to her father, and when he'd finished, her mother said, 'There isn't anything to connect you with David's dealings, and Saul will soon sort it out.'

'But there is, Mum! He's a family friend, and as far as Saul is concerned, he could have given me information.' Bonzo, who had decided that this resting place was too agitated, jumped off and stalked out of the room.

Mrs Sharland smiled at her daughter. 'They can examine your record minutely, and I know they won't find anything wrong. Now, I could do with a nice strong cup of tea. That stuff your Aunt Grace makes is indescribable.'

Jane watched her walk out of the room, seeming quite unperturbed by the turn of events. 'Why wasn't I born with some of her confidence that everything will turn out right in the end?'

A deep chuckle came from her father. 'She's always been the same, but she is right, you know, Jane. And has it occurred to you that you might have jumped to the wrong conclusion?'

'What do you mean?'

'Think about it calmly for a moment. Saul didn't actually accuse you of insider dealing, did he?'

'No, as I've already told you, he never came right out and said that, but he didn't like the fact that I'd bought those shares, and he told me to come home and stay here.'

'He might not have wanted to distress you with the details as they wound up the investigation.'

She shook her head as the doubts crept in. Was her father right? 'I don't know, Dad. I just wish he'd explained, but he went back into his office and closed the door.'

At that moment her mother returned with a tray of tea and mince pies. 'I expect this distressing business is why the dear man said he couldn't come this evening.' She handed out the cups. 'I'll just phone him and say that we understand, but he must still come, no matter how late it is.'

Her husband leapt to his feet, nearly sending the cup flying, and took the phone out of his wife's hand. 'You mustn't interfere.'

She look crestfallen and sat down again. 'I'm not a fool,' she told him, 'but it upsets me to see Jane so worried. I just wanted to talk to him, that's all.'

'He can't tell you anything at this stage,' he told his wife gently. 'We'll just have to wait and see what happens.'

'I suppose your right.' She smiled brightly again. 'He knows what he's doing, and anyway, he's in love with our daughter and nothing is going to stop him from eliminating her from this wretched affair.'

Jane's mouth dropped open in astonishment. 'How did you come to that conclusion?'

'Oh, it's quite obvious,' her mother told her. 'I knew it as soon as I saw you together. The poor man must be in turmoil and I'm not surprised he wants you out of the way for a while.'

'I don't believe this,' Jane breathed. Her mother was a romantic at heart, but this notion was beyond belief.

'Andrew's got himself a girlfriend,' her mother announced. 'Which is just as well, because he couldn't have Jane now. Saul would never allow it.'

'Mother!'

'Don't look so outraged, my dear. I know you're attracted to him; I saw the way your were looking at him.'

'Well, yes I am,' she admitted, 'but he thinks I'm a criminal.'

'Of course he doesn't.' The idea was instantly dismissed. 'I expect he just wants to save you from any unpleasantness.'

'But, Mum, how can you sound so positive?'

'It's quite simple, Jane, if he'd had any proof of your guilt then he would have called the police, not told you to go home. And anyway, he wouldn't have come here last night if he'd had an inkling that you were involved in anything underhand.' Her mother looked highly pleased with her logic.

'You don't know anything about the business world,' Jane pointed out.

'I agree.' She smiled at her husband. 'I left college and married your father right away so I never went out to work, but I do know people, and my instinct tells me that Saul Devlin is an honourable man, and he won't let anything bad happen to you.'

'I hope you're right.' Jane gave up the argument. All she could do now was wait.

They'd had a busy evening, with their neighbours from both sides, Andrew and his new girlfriend, and Aunt Agnes, round for tea. Now they had all left and Jane and her parents were enjoying a hot drink before retiring. It was one o'clock in the morning when the doorbell rang.

'Someone's forgotten something,' her father sighed and went to see who it was.

He didn't reappear for some time, and there was the sound of voices talking earnestly.

Her mother yawned. 'You'd think they'd talked enough tonight. I don't think we've ever had such a noisy crowd.'

'It was a good party, Mum. Everyone enjoyed themselves.'

Mrs Sharland looked at her daughter speculatively. 'But did you?'

She nodded. 'Yes, I managed to push the worry to the back of my mind for a while. It wasn't easy, but I think I must have overreacted; Saul can't possibly think I have been in league with David, and my record will confirm that.'

'Of course it will.' Her mother looked sad. 'I managed to get hold of David this morning, and he admitted that he was under investigation.'

'That's awful.' Jane wiped a tear from her eyes. 'I would never have believed him capable of doing such a thing.'

'Well, it's hard to know what drives some people. Let's just hope that the bank is wrong and David is innocent.' She smiled encouragingly at her daughter and changed the subject. 'What did you think of Andrew's girl?'

'She seemed very pleasant. I would say they are extremely well suited.'

'She won't ruffle the waters of his ordered life, you mean?' her mother asked, perceptively.

Jane nodded. 'Exactly.'

'Look who's here,' her father said, coming into the room at last.

Jane leapt to her feet when she saw the tall figure of Saul.

'I'm sorry to call at this late hour,' he apologised, 'but I wanted to see Jane.'

'Of course you did.' Her mother eyed

the big man thoughtfully. 'You look exhausted. Have you had anything to eat today?'

'Not much,' he admitted. 'I've been too busy.'

'Well sit down.' Saul received a sympathetic smile. 'It won't take long to fix you a meal. That tie suits you, I knew it would.' Then she was gone.

Bonzo recognised a friendly sleeping place and leapt onto Saul as soon as he sat in the chair. Jane watched him stroking the cat in the same distracted way she had done earlier in the day.

'Have you completed your investigation?' her father asked.

'Yes, not only has a bank employee been insider dealing, he has also been embezzling funds.'

Jane gasped, this was even worse than she had feared. 'David?'

He nodded. 'It will soon be public knowledge. He has been charged and released on bail until the trial.'

'What about me?'

Saul gave her a bland look. 'You want

to be arrested as well?'

'No, I don't!' When her father began to laugh, she looked from one man to the other. It took her a while to realise what was going on, and she wasn't usually this slow on the uptake.

'I've been worrying myself sick,' she exploded, 'and you're making jokes about it?'

Saul was on his feet, spilling an irritable cat onto the floor, and pulling her out of the chair. 'May I see your daughter on her own, Mr Sharland?'

'Of course. I'll just go and give my wife a hand in the kitchen.'

When they were alone she looked into his eyes and begged, 'Please tell me what's going on.'

'When I had all the facts, Brandon was interviewed and charged. He didn't try to deny anything, in fact, he admitted that he was only trying to get some extra money for his retirement.'

'But what about the shares I bought?'

'Oh, those.' He pulled her towards him and kissed her gently. 'Bad judgement on your part - the bank are not going to be pleased.'

'What are you talking about?' She was getting disorientated, his hand was caressing her spine and making her legs go weak. She tried to gather her scattered wits; she must concentrate. 'Isn't that company going to make a dramatic recovery?'

'Nope. The shares will probably go up a little when trading starts in the New Year, so your losses might not be too bad after all.'

'How do you know all this?'

'I've been talking to the Managing Director today.' He pushed a strand of hair away from her face.

'What, on Boxing Day?'

His smile was wry. 'I've spoilt quite a few people's holiday this year.'

She caught hold of his tormenting hands. 'But David bought them as well.'

'Biggest blunder he ever made, he told me.'

Releasing his hands she relaxed in his arms with a sigh of relief, then she remembered something. 'But you suspected me of wrong doing!'

'No, I didn't.' He looked shocked.

She leant back until she could look him in the eyes. 'Oh, come on! You made me leave this morning.'

'I did that because I was about to get the police involved and things were going to get unpleasant for someone you knew and had obviously liked. I soon cleared up any doubt that you might have received some information from Brandon and acted on it, but if you'd stayed you would have seen the evidence of what Brandon had done.'

'Were you afraid I would phone and warn him to get out of the country?'

'Of course not.' He nibbled her ear, and she pushed him away, reluctantly.

'Then why didn't you tell me all this instead of letting me worry?' She wasn't going to let him get away with this. She needed an explanation.

'I couldn't, darling. The fraud was only just coming to light and I had a lot of people to contact.'

Er ... did he call her darling?

'You must understand,' he said earnestly, 'that I had to check every tiny detail.'

She smiled then; her father had been right to tell her that she must trust him. 'I'm glad you did.'

He kissed her again. 'I knew the woman I love could never be a criminal.'

'L … love? But you've only just met me.'

'Time has nothing to do with it. As soon as you walked into my office I knew you were the woman I wanted to spend the rest of my life with.'

'Did you?' she asked in wonder, not being able to believe this was happening.

'Yes, did you feel the same?' For the first time he looked uncertain.

'No, I took an instant dislike to you,' she told him with a laugh.

'Well, I hope to goodness that you've changed your mind, because I have no intention of letting you out of my sight.'

'It quickly turned to love,' she assured him.

He let out a pent-up breath. 'Thank

heavens for that. I've never believed in love at first sight, but that was what happened to me as soon as I saw you. I knew I had to keep you with me so we could get to know each other quickly, because in a few days I would be leaving and might never see you again.'

'Is that why you made me work for you?'

He nodded and gazed at her seriously. 'I took a big gamble relieving you of your work, but it seemed the only option open to me.'

'You mean my mistake wasn't bad enough to make me lose my job?' She was beginning to understand what had happened.

'Of course not. The job is still yours …' He paused, 'that's if you want it?'

She pretended to consider for a moment, then beamed at him. 'I'm not sure.'

'Good, because I've got another position for you.'

'Oh? As your secretary?'

'Certainly not! I happen to know that

the Edinburgh branch of the bank is headhunting for a good dealer. Someone who knows the markets well. It'll be more money too. I can recommend you, if you'd like…?'

Her eyes shone. 'But wouldn't that mean…?'

'This job does come with some strings, I'm afraid. It will involve some serious commitment.' He took a deep breath and smiled in the way that had melted her heart right from the beginning. 'Will you marry me, Jane?'

She wrapped her arms around him with a gurgle of joy. 'Yes, please.'

'I'm going back to Scotland in two days' time and I want you to come with me. I'm not going to let you out of my sight,' he told her huskily.

Just before he started to kiss her again, she caught a glimpse of her mother, pushing her husband out of the door, with a huge smile on her face.

Jane sighed contentedly and showed Saul just how much she loved him. What had started as a crisis had turned out to be the best Christmas ever.

THE END

If you enjoyed this Barley Book Handbag Romance, why not try some other titles in the series:

Links of Love by Beryl Matthews
I.S.B.N.: 1902691113

An Echo in Time by Kate O'Neill
1902691164

Manhattan Magicby Laura Hart
I.S.B.N.:1902691024

Love Restored by Lindy Benton
I.S.B.N.:1902691016

Better the Devil … by Andrea Presneill
I.S.B.N.:1902691105

The Gold-diggers by Charlotte Brooke
I.S.B.N.:1902691008

The books are available in your local bookstore and also from:

www.barleybooks.co.uk,

or direct from:

Barley Books
P.O. Box 103
Leeds LS169YD

Sales: 0151 632 2822